LAURA'S LOVE
LETTERS UNLIMITED

LAURA'S LOVE
LETTERS UNLIMITED

RAY JONES

All glory to God.

CONTENTS

LOVE LETTERS UNLIMITED

THESE LOVE LETTERS ARE THOSE LETTERS
THAT THEATRICALLY
SPEAK
THE THOUGHTS THAT THUNDER
THROUGH MY HEART WHICH THERAPEUTICALLY
REPEATS
WHAT I FEEL FOR LAURA
WHEN ALL THE THOUGHTS OF LAURA
MENTALLY GATHER IN MY BRAIN
THE GENETICS THAT PROVIDE
THIS DREAM LIKE HAYRIDE
IS THE GIFT MY HEART CONTAINS

LOVE LETTERS UNLIMITED
WRITINGS THAT COMES TO ME AT WILL
EMOTIONS THAT TWIST AND TURN INSIDE
THAT ULTIMATELY REVEALS
THAT THESE LOVE LETTERS
ARE THE LOVE LETTERS
A NATURAL OCCURRENCE TAKES PLACE
WHEN MY WIFE AND I
LOOK AND SEE EYE TO EYE
IS NOTHING LESS THAN AMAZING GRACE

THESE ARE THE LETTERS
THE PRICELESS TREASURES
MEMORIES THAT WILL BE APART
ALWAYS BRING PLEASURE
THAT WILL BE WITH ME FOREVER
WITH PERMANT RESIDENCY IN MY HEART

LOVE LETTERS UNLIMTITED
WILL CONTINUE TO FLOURISH AND RELAY
THE LOVE THAT LAURA SEEMS TO INSPIRE
IN ME EACH AND EVERY DAY

BLESSED

GOD HAS BEEN VERY GRATEFUL
BY BLESSING US AGAIN
WITH SO MUCH JOY AND LOVE
FOR SOME CAN'T COMPREHEND

IT SEEMED A LONG TIME COMING
BUT OUR PRAYERS WERE ALWAYS HEARD
EVEN THOUGH THE MOUNTAIN WAS STEEP
WE CLIMBED TOGETHER WHILE HE OBSERVED

HE SAW THE SUPPORT WE GAVE EACH OTHER
AND KNEW LOVE WOULD NEVER END
HE KNEW WE'D CONTINUE TO PURSUE
UNTIL HE BLESSED US ONCE AGAIN

TO BE GRATEFUL SEEMS SO LITTLE
TO BE FREE OF SIN IS IMPOSSIBLE TO DO
BUT I WILL CONTINUE TO PRAISE THE LORD ABOVE
AS I WILL CONTINUE ON LOVING YOU

LAURA YOU ARE TO BE CHERISHED
I AM THE CHERRIES IN WHICH TO BE USED
TO GIVE YOU A LIFE TIME OF PLEASURES
WITH NO MINUTES OR SECONDS TO LOSE

GOD HAS BEEN VERY GRATEFUL
BY BLESSING US AGAIN
WITH EVERLASTING LOVE FOR ONE ANOTHER
AND ANOTHER LOVE TO COMPREHEND

AMAZING

ISN'T IT AMAZING
THE FEELINGS THAT ARE THERE
THE UNLIMITED AMOUNT OF LOVE
THAT WE SHARE AS A PAIR

THE UNLIMITED AMOUNT OF LOVE
THAT GROWS STRONGER EVERYDAY
AND LOVING ONE ANOTHER
IS THE ONLY PRICE WE PAY

ISN'T IT AMAZING
TO BE BLESSED LIKE THIS
TO LOVE EACH OTHER NATURALLY
THEN SEAL IT WITH A KISS

THE UNLIMITED AMOUNT OF LOVE
THAT MONEY CANNOT BUY
PRICELESS, UNBELIEVABLE
A LOVE THAT I HOLD HIGH

I LOVE YOU MY DARLING
I SAY THAT WITH WORDS THAT I CAN TASTE
OUR LOVE IS GODS GIFT TO US
THIS IS OUR AMAZING GRACE

LOVE ON MY MIND

I KNOW I HAVE'NT WRITTEN YOU
A POEM IN A LONG TIME
BUT THAT DOES NOT MEAN I DON'T HAVE
OUR LOVE ON MY MIND

OUR LOVE STAYS ON MY MIND
EVEN MORE WHEN WERE APART
BECAUSE YOU'RE SINCERE WHEN YOU'RE NEAR
AND THAT'S DEAR TO MY HEART

THIS IS A NEW YEAR
AND WE HAVE SO MANY DAYS AHEAD
TO FIND OUT IF OUR LOVE IS ON THE RIGHT TRACK
OR TO FIND OUT IF IT'S BEING MISLEAD

OUR LOVE FEELS SO WEALTHY AND RIGHT
SO HOW CAN IT BE WRONG
IF IT WASN'T MEANT TO BE
IT WOULDN'T HAVE LASTED THIS LONG

CONSIDERING THE CIRCUMSTANCES
I THINK WE PASS THE TEST
AND SHOULD WE CONTINUE TO SEE ONE ANOTHER
I THINK THAT WOULD BE BEST

MAY OUR LOVE CONTINUE TO GROW
AND MAY YOU NEVER SHED A TEAR
I WILL ALWAYS LOVE YOU FOREVER
HAVE A HEALTHY AND HAPPY NEW YEAR

FOOD FOR THOUGHT

I LOVE YOU

SINCE WE'VE BEEN MARRIED
MY LIFE HAS BEEN GREAT
YOU COOK DINNER FOR ME
WHICH IS YOUR LOVE TO ME ON A PLATE

AS WE SIT AND EAT TOGETHER
I FORGET I'M STARING AT YOU
WHAT I'M DOING IS ADMIRING YOUR BEAUTY
AND HOW GREAT YOUR COOKING IS TOO

WILL IT ALWAYS BE LIKE THIS
THE MAGIC THAT WE SHARE
THE LOVE OF ALL LOVES
NO OTHER CAN COMPARE

SO EVERY TIME WE EAT TOGETHER
AND YOU REALIZE I'M STARING AT YOU
IT'S NOT BECAUSE SOMETHING IS WRONG
IT'S BECAUSE YOU MADE MY DREAMS COME TRUE

JUST FOR THE RECORD

JUST FOR THE RECORD HONEY
I LOVE YOU
I'LL SAY IT OVER AND OVER AGAIN
I'LL LOVE YOU THROUGH AN ENDLESS DAY
AND EVEN MORE WHEN THE DAY BEGINS

JUST FOR THE RECORD HONEY
I LOVE YOU
YOU'RE ALL I NEED AND MORE
BEFORE I MET YOU I ONLY LOVED
A COUPLE OF HOURS A DAY
NOW I LOVE FOR TWENTY-FOUR

JUST FOR THE RECORD LET IT BE KNOWN
THAT MY LOVE FOR YOU HONEY HAS GROWN
EXPANDING IN SO MANY WAYS
LIKE LOVING YOU THROUGH ENDLESS DAYS

JUST FOR THE RECORD
YOU ARE MY WIFE
AND I'M YOUR HUSBAND
UNTIL THE END OF LIFE
AFTER THAT WE CAN BEGIN
LOVING EACH OTHER ALL OVER AGAIN

STILLED LOVE

ISN'T IT AMAZING, HOW MUCH I STILL LOVE YOU
MY LOVE FOR YOU JUST KEEPS GROWING STRONGER
I WAS THE LONELIEST MAN IN THE WORLD
BUT TODAY I'M LONELY NO LONGER

YOU ARE EVERYTHING AND THE WORLD TO ME
MY WIFE MY LOVER AND FRIEND
WITHOUT YOU MY LIFE HAS NO MEANING
THE WORLD AS I KNOW IT WOULD END

YOU ARE ALWAYS BEAUTIFUL TO ME
EVEN IN THE DARKEST NIGHT
AND IF MY EYES SHOULD FAIL ME TOMORROW
MY HEART WOULD BE MY SIGHT

IT'S WONDERFUL HOW MUCH I STILL LOVE
AS TIME JUST KEEPS PASSING BY
NEVER FORGET THAT
I'LL LOVE YOU EVEN MORE TOMORROW
STILL LOVE IN MY HEART I CAN'T DENY

WITH GODS HELP

I'LL ALWAYS BE HERE FOR HER
I KNEW IT THE FIRST TIME WE MET
THAT SHE WOULD BECOME MY INSPIRATION
HER NAME WAS LAURA, I'D NEVER FORGET

THEN EARTHLY PRESSURES WERE BESTOWED UPON ME
THE DEVIL OTHERS MAY SAY
SAID FORGET THAT NEW FOUND FEELING OF LOVE
AND LET THAT LAURA BE ON HER WAY

IMPOSSIBLE! MY FEELING SAID TO ME
WITH EVERY BEAT OF MY HEART
TRUE LOVE IS RARER THAN DIAMONDS
SO FOR ONCE IN YOUR LIFE BE SMART

THE ODDS WERE STACKED AGAINST ME
AS HIGH AS THE EYE COULD SEE
BUT LUCKILY I WEAR GLASSES
AND I'M AS BLIND AS I CAN BE

SO TO THE DEVIL I PAID NO ATTENTION
IGNORED HIM OTHERS MIGHT SAY
THIS IS MY BEGINNING TO HAPPINESS
AND I'LL LET NOTHING GET IN MY WAY

THIS WAS HARDER THAN I IMAGINED
AND SOME SAY LOVE IS GRAND
I REACHED OUT FOR SOMEONE TO HELP ME
BUT NO ONE WOULD LEND A HAND

AT TIMES I FELT I WAS FALLING
AWAY FROM MY TRUE LOVE
IN REALITY WE WERE GETTING CLOSER
LIKE A HAND INSIDE A GLOVE

FINALLY THE TIME HAD COME
I FELT I HAD TO MAKE A STAND
I BENT DOWN ON ONE KNEE
AND ASKED LAURA FOR HER HAND

I LOVE YOU, WILL YOU MARRY ME
I HAD MY FINGERS CROSSED
FOR IF SHE SAID THAT SHE WASN'T READY
ALL I DREAMED OF WOULD BE LOST

I'LL ALWAYS BE HERE FOR HER
EVEN AFTER MY EARTHLY LIFE
SO FOR NOW WERE LIVING IN HAPPINESS
LAURA IS NOW MY WIFE.

NEVER ENDING LOVE

GOD ONCE SAID TO ME, THAT WE SHOULD BE ONE
SO THEN IT WAS WRITTEN, AND NOW IT IS DONE

WHEN I LOOK INTO THE SKY I SEE BLUE
WHEN I LOOK INTO MY HEART
I SEE MY LOVE FOR YOU
AND EVEN IF I CLOSE MY EYES, I SEE
A NEVER ENDING ROAD OF LOVE
AND HAPPINESS FOR YOU AND ME

BUT EVERY MINUTE THAT WERE APART
MY HEART MISSES YOU AS IF IT WERE TWO
BUT EVERY MOMENT THAT WERE TOGETHER
MY HEART PUMPS DOUBLE LOVE FOR YOU

AS THE DAYS CONTINUE TO MOVE ON
MY LOVE FOR YOU WILL REMAIN SHARP AS A THORN
I'M SURE I WILL ALWAYS FEEL THIS WAY
AS TIME PASSES DAY BY DAY

WEEK TO WEEK MONTH TO MONTH YEAR TO YEAR
I KNEW IT WAS YOU WHOM I WAS TO MARRY MY DEAR
WE'LL RAISE A FAMILY AND HAPPY WE'LL BE
AND CONTINUE TO LOVE EACH OTHER ETERNALLY

WHAT I'M REALLY TRYING TO SAY TO YOU
IS THAT I'LL NEVER REGRET SAYING I DO
AND IF I HAD TO REPEAT OUR WEDDING VOW
I COULDN'T LOVE YOU ANY MORE THAN I LOVE YOU NOW

BACK AND FORTH

WE ARE BECOMING ONE
IN ALL THAT WE DO
I THINK OUR LOVE IS SPECIAL
I CAN'T HELP FROM LOVING YOU

I LOVED YOU YESTERDAY
AND I'LL ALWAYS LOVE YOU TOMORROW
THE LOVE I FEEL FOR YOU
IN THIS WORLD YOU CAN NOT BORROW

TODAY I CAN'T HELP BUT WONDER
IF TOMORROW, WILL I BE AROUND
SO TODAY ALL I CAN DO IS TREASURE
THE LOVE THAT YOU AND I FOUND

YESTERDAY WAS BEAUTIFUL
THE BEST THAT IT COULD BE
TOMORROW WILL BE LOVELIER
AS LONG AS YOU'RE WITH ME

I COULD GO ON FOREVER
BUT YESTERDAY IS COMING TO AN END
I'M SO GLAD I HAVE TOMORROW
TO CONTINUE LOVING YOU AGAIN

YESTERDAY HAS ALWAYS BEEN BEAUTIFUL
SINCE THE DAY WE SAID I DO
TOMORROW I HOPE WILL NEVER END
AS LONG AS I'M MARRIED TO YOU

DREAMS OF YOU

THIS IS TO THE WOMAN I DREAM OF
LUCKILY I MARRIED HER
AND WE'RE WONDERFULLY IN LOVE

I USE TO DREAM OF YOU
IN THE MIDDLE OF THE NIGHT
AND THE DREAMS JUST CARRIED ON
LIKE A PEACEFUL DOVE IN FLIGHT

I NEVER REALLY WONDERED
WHETHER DREAMS REALLY CAME TRUE
UNTIL I SAW YOU WALKING DOWN THE ISLE
AND I ACTUALLY MARRIED YOU

BEFORE THERE WAS DARKNESS
AND IN MY DREAMS I'D WEEP
YOU BRIGHTENED UP MY DREAMS
AND NOW I SMILE WHEN I SLEEP

ITS WONDERFUL BEING MARRIED
AND EVEN MORE TO YOU
I AM THE HAPPIEST MAN IN THE WORLD
BECAUSE A DREAM OF MINE CAME TRUE

LAURA WITH CHILD

WHAT WILL SHE BE LIKE
I WONDER, I GUESS
MY SMILE YOUR EYES
WITH BABY SOFT FLESH

WE WILL BE GOOD PARENTS
GOOD PARENTS WE WILL BE
AS LONG AS I HAVE YOU
AS LONG AS YOU HAVE ME

WHAT WILL WE FEEL WHEN
SHE STARTS TO CRY
NERVOUS, UNSURE
WITH TEARS IN HER EYE

WILL SHE EAT ALL HER VEGGIES
DRINK ALL HER MILK
GROW UP TO LIKE COTTONS
INSTEAD OF SILKS

WHO WILL SHE BE LIKE
YOUR SISTER MY BROTHER
WHAT WOULD REALLY MAKE ME HAPPY
IF SHE'S JUST LIKE HER MOTHER

UNBORN

THE CHILD INSIDE OF YOU
WILL SOON COME OUT
WITH NEEDS AND DESIRES
WITH BELIEFS AND DOUTS

SHE'LL DEPEND ON US
TO GUIDE HER THROUGH
HER UPS AND DOWNS
THE GOALS SHE'LL PURSUE

WE SHALL TEACH HER TO LOVE
WITH THE LOVE THAT WE SHARE
KNOWING WE ARE BLESSED
WITH A LOVE THAT IS RARE

OUR LITTLE MIRICALE
OUR UNBORN CHILD
WITH LOVE IN HER HEART
AND A FACE WITH A SMILE

FEELINGS CHANGE

MY FEELINGS FOR YOU ARE CHANGING
I NEVER THOUGHT THEY COULD
THEIR CHANGING FOR THE BETTER
GOD MADE SURE THEY WOULD

IT'S AMAZING HOW THINGS HAPPEN
I'M STARTING TO LOVE YOU MORE
IT'S GREAT HAVING THESE FEELINGS
FOR THE WIFE THAT I ADORE

MY FEELING HAVE NEVER FELT BETTER
THEY FEEL LOVED WHEN YOU ARE NEAR
THEY ALSO FEEL THEY WILL LOVE YOU MORE
THIS SAME DAY AND TIME NEXT YEAR

MY FEELINGS FOR YOU ARE CHANGING
AS TIME JUST PASSES BY
MY LOVE FOR YOU GROWS GREATER
AND I'LL NEVER QUESTION WHY

BRAIN STORMING

I'M SITTING HERE INSIDE MYSELF
THINKING ABOUT YOU AS I DO
AND WONDERING ABOUT THE HARD TIMES
THAT THE DEVIL PUT US THROUGH

HE CAN ONLY GET TO US LAURA
WHEN WE'VE BEEN APART
HE CAN NEVER COME BETWEEN US
WHEN WE'RE TOGETHER HEART TO HEART

RIGHT NOW WE'RE SACRIFICING BEING TOGETHER
BECAUSE THERE'S SOMETHING WE MUST DO
TO MAKE A BETTER FUTURE FOR US
AND FOR OUR CHILDREN TOO

THINGS WILL NATURALLY GET BETTER
BECAUSE TRUE LOVE ALWAYS PREVAILS
AND WHAT WE HAVE IS REAL LOVE
NOT JUST SOME FAIRY TALE

I'M SITTING HERE INSIDE MYSELF
LOVING YOU AS I ALWAYS DO
AND SMILING ABOUT THE GREAT TIMES
GOD IS BESTOWING UPON ME AND YOU

YOUR SWEETNESS IS MY WEAKNESS

YOUR SWEETNESS IS MY WEAKNESS
SO CHOCOLATE MEANS NOTHING TO ME
YOU ARE SWEETER THAN THE FINEST CHOCOLATE
FRESH OUT OF WILLIES FACTORY

I NEVER RECALL HAVING A SWEET TOOTH
UNTIL YOU CAME IN MY LIFE
NOW THIS UNCONTROLLABLE URGE FOR YOU'RE SWEETNESS
THAT'S WHY I ASKED YOU TO BE MY WIFE

THEY SAY TOO MUCH SUGAR IS NOT GOOD FOR YOU
BUT I OVERDOSE ON YOU EVERYDAY
TO ME YOU'RE WHAT SUGAR EVOLVED FROM
LAURA, YOUR SWEETNESS JUST BLOWS ME AWAY

ALL DAY I'M BRIGHT EYED AND BUSHY TAILED
PEOPLE CAN'T SEEM TO SEE
THAT THE REASON THAT I'M ALWAYS JOYOUS
IS THAT YOUR SWEETNESS FLOWS CONSTANTLY THROUGH ME

YOUR SWEETNESS IS MY WEAKNESS
THEY SAY YOU ARE WHAT YOU EAT
AND I'LL ALWAYS EAT YOU'RE SWEETNESS
FOR ME THERE'S NO OTHER SWEET TREAT

LOVE ME THROUGH OUR PROBLEMS

HELLO MY LOVELY WIFE
THESE PAST FEW DAYS, COMMUNICATION HAS BEEN WEAK
IS IT BECAUSE OUR ANNIVERSARY IS UPON US
AT THE END OF THIS UNUSUAL WEEK

REMEMBER THINGS CAN'T ALWAYS BE GREAT BETWEEN US
IT'S TIMES LIKE THIS WE HAVE TO WORK THROUGH
THERE'S NO OTHERS THAT CAN COMPARE TO YOU BABY
THAT'S WHY I MARRIED YOU

I LOVE YOU MORE THROUGH OUR DIFFICULT TIMES
THAT'S WHAT KEEPS ME FROM GOING ASTRAY
JUST BECAUSE WE HAD TOUGH TIMES YESTERDAY
DOESN'T MEAN WE WILL HAVE THEM TODAY

SO REMEMBER THAT I ALWAYS LOVE YOU
FROM MONDAY TO SUNDAY
FROM A TO Z
YOU ARE MY GUIDING LIGHT
AND MY SHINNING STAR
YOU ARE THE WORLD TO ME

PROBLEMS JUST MAKE ME STRONGER
TO LOVE YOU MORE EACH DAY
SO LETS MAKE OUR PROBLEMS POSITIVE
AND BE HAPPILY ON OUR WAY

APOLOGY

JEALOUS OF ANOTHER MAN
YES I WAS JEALOUS I MOST CONFESS
I WANT TO BE THE ONLY MAN THAT MAKES YOU LAUGH
IS THAT JEALOUSY OR SELFISHNESS

YOU KNOW YOU ARE THE WORLD TO ME
TO SHARE YOU I GUESS I MUST
SO I WILL RELINQUISH YOU A LITTLE WITH AN OPEN MIND
FILLED WITH LOVE LOYALTY AND TRUST

WHO WANTS TO SHARE HIS BEAUTIFUL WIFE
WITH A WORLD THAT WON'T SHARE BACK
TO BE SELFISH WITH A WIFE AS GLAMOROUS AS YOU
WILL CAUSE ME TO HAVE A HEART ATTACK

TO ME YOU'RE A VULNERABLE VIRGIN
IN A WORLD WITH MEN HORNY AS CAN BE
AND JEALOUSY IS A NEGATIVE EMOTION
THAT SHOWS INSECURITY

JEALOUS OF ANOTHER MAN
YES I WAS JEALOUS I CONFESS
BUT ONLY BECAUSE I LOVE YOU DEARLY
FOR YOU DESERVE NOTHING LESS

I'M THANKFUL

LOVE IS SPLENDID
TO BE LOVED IS GREAT
TO LOVE YOU IS EVEN GREATER
NO WEALTH CAN COMPENSATE

FOR THE LOVE WE HAVE MY DEAR
FOR THE FEELINGS THAT ARE SERENE
FOR THE WAY THAT WE GAZE INTO EACH OTHERS EYES
LET NOTHING EVER INTERVENE

WITH THE LOVE THAT WILL CONTINUE TO GROW BETWEEN US
WITH THE EMOTIONS THAT WE BOTH SHARE
OUR HEARTS WILL ALWAYS BEAT AS ONE
GOD KNOWS THAT LOVE IS THERE

LOVING YOU IS SPLENDID
TOUCHING YOU IS DIVINE
HOW LUCKY CAN A HUSBAND BE
TO HAVE YOU'RE BEAUTY, YOU'RE BODY AND YOU'RE MIND

WIFE WITH CHILD

LIVING IN STILL WATER
BREATHING LIQUID AIR
PROTECTED FROM POLLUTION
WITH ONLY LOVE AND CARE

WAITING FOR THE MOMENT
WHEN THE LIGHT WILL HIT YOUR EYE
ENTERING THE WORLD NUDE
WITH NO REASON TO BE SHY

BEING CLOSE TO YOU AND YOUR MOTHER
WITH A WARM FEELING INSIDE
EXPERIENCING A NEW KIND OF LOVE
ANOTHER LOVE I CANNOT HIDE

HOLDING YOU IN MY ARMS
WITH ONLY THOUGHTS OF YOU
WILL FILL MY EYES WITH WATER
FOR I AM HOLDING YOU'RE MOTHER TOO

LIVING IN STILL WATER
BREATHING LIQUID AIR
BEING ONE WITH YOU AND YOU'RE MOTHER
A FEELING I LOVE TO SHARE

MORE ROOM FOR LOVING YOU

ANOTHER ROOM TO LOVE YOU IN
THAT'S WHAT WERE GOING TO BUILD
WE CAN'T SUPPLY IT WITH FURNITURE AT THIS TIME
BUT WITH LOVE IT CAN BE FILLED

THROUGH OUT EVERY CRACK AND CREVICE
HAPPINESS WILL FILL THE ROOM
THIS ROOM WILL HOLD NO SORROW
THIS ROOM WILL HOLD NO GLOOM

WE WILL BUILD THIS ROOM WITH PRICELESS EMOTIONS
THAT COMES STRAIGHT FROM THE HEART
THIS ROOM WILL BE VERY VALUABLE TO US
LET ANGER NEVER TEAR IT APART

WE WILL SHARE THIS ROOM WITH OUR CHILDREN
TEACH THEM ABOUT THE LOVE THAT FILLS THE AIR
SHOW THEM THE LOVE THAT WE HAVE FOR ONE ANOTHER
EVEN THROUGH HEARTACHE AND DESPAIR

ANOTHER ROOM TO LOVE YOU IN MY DARLING
WHEN OUR ROOM IS FINALLY COMPLETE
WE WILL CELEBRATE WITH DINNER BY CANDLE LIGHT
AND FOR DESSERT I'LL HAVE YOU MY SWEET

HOME IS WHERE MY WIFE IS

A HOUSE IS NOT A HOME
WHEN MY WIFE IS NOT THERE
IT'S JUST MANY ROOMS FILLED WITH FURNITURE
WHICH IN NO WAY CAN COMPARE

SHE FILLS OUR HOUSE WITH LOVE
LIKE NO ONE ELSE CAN DO
SHE FILLS MY HEART THE SAME
EVERYDAY AND ALL YEAR THROUGH

A HOUSE IS NOT A HOME
IF MY WIFE IS NOT HERE WITH ME
IT'S JUST A MASS OF SUBSTANCE
WITH AIR AND A COLOR TV

BUT DO NOT GET ME WRONG
INDEED I LOVE MY HOUSE
THOUGH MY HOUSE IS NOT A HOME
IF IT DOESN'T CONTAIN MY SPOUSE

THE DARKNESS

THE DARKNESS NEVER LAST
WHILE LOVE IS IN THE HEART
WHEN TIMES SEEM THEIR DARKNESS
BE PATIENT, THE DARKNESS WILL DEPART

LOVE HAS A WAY OF CONQUERING
IF WE EXHAUST ALL OTHER MEANS
THOUGH THE DARKNESS BRINGS DIRT UPON US
LOVE QUICKLY COMES AND CLEANS

THE DARKNESS IS VERY POWERFUL
IT TAKES AWAY ONES SIGHT
BUT TRUE LOVE IS EVEN STRONGER
FOR THROUGH OUR HEARTS WE SEE THE LIGHT

THE LOVE WE HAVE LAURA IS SPECIAL
WHEN THE DARKNESS GETS IN THE WAY
JUST CLOSE YOUR EYES AND FEEL OUR LOVE
IT SHALL BRING US A BRIGHTER DAY

THE DARKNESS IS DIMINISHING
IT WILL COME AND IT WILL GO
OUR LOVE WILL REMAIN DOMINANT
OVER THE DARKNESS
THIS I SURELY KNOW

WONDERFUL SECRET

THE SECRET WE SHARE
I MUST CONFESS
IT'S A WONDERFUL SECRET
MATTER OF FACT IT'S THE BEST

THE SECRET WAS CONCEIVED
BETWEEN TWO LOVERS, YOU AND I
EITHER DAY OR NIGHT
ON THE FOURTH OF JULY

THE SECRET YOU KNOW
AGAIN ITS CALLED LOVE
BUT ON A DIFFERENT LEVEL
ONE WE ALWAYS DREAM OF

WE TRIED SO HARD
FOR THIS DREAM COME TRUE
THIS WONDERFUL SECRET
BETWEEN ME AND YOU

THIS SECRET WE SHARE
ONE DAY MUST BE TOLD
TO OUR FAMILY AND FRIENDS
THE YOUNG AND THE OLD

THEY DESERVE THE RIGHT
TO KNOW ABOUT OUR LIFE
AND THE SECRET WE SHARE
AS HUSBAND AND WIFE

IS THERE MORE OF YOU TO LOVE
OR DO I LOVE YOU MORE
BECAUSE OF THE SECRET
WE CONCEIVED ON THE FLOOR

LET'S SAY HELLO TO AUGUST
AND FAREWELL TO JULY
WHICH GAVE US THIS SECRET
BETWEEN YOU AND I

I LOVE YOU AND MY SECRET
I MUST CONFESS,
LAURA YOU ARE THE WORLD TO ME
THANK GOD I'VE BEEN BLESSED.

I LOVE YOU BABY, ALL OF YOU

TELLING YOU

HAVE I TOLD YOU HOW HAPPY I AM
LOVING YOU DAY BY DAY
KNOWING THAT YOU ARE MY WIFE
AND HAVING A BABY ON THE WAY

HAVE I TOLD YOU HOW BLESSED I FEEL
THAT YOU CHOSE TO MARRY ME
IN SICKNESS AND IN HEALTH
THROUGHOUT ETERNITY

HAVE I TOLD YOU HOW THANKFUL I AM
THAT YOU WILL ALWAYS BE BY MY SIDE
AND AS A REPAYMENT FOR YOUR LOVE AND LOYALTY
MY EVER LASTING LOVE THAT WILL NEVER SUBSIDE

HAVE I TOLD YOU WHAT YOU MEAN TO ME
YOU MEAN HAPPINESS LIFE REBORN
YOU ARE MY LUNGS AND MY OXYGEN
WITH OUT YOU I CAN'T GO ON

HAVE I TOLD YOU THAT I LOVE YOU
I DO I DO I DO
LOVE YOU I DO
LOVE YOU I DO FOREVER ME AND YOU

DEBRA'S INSPIRATION

DAMN LAURA'S HAVING MY BABY
IS THIS WHAT LIFE IS ALL ABOUT
A BABY GIRL INSIDE MY WIFE
WAITING TO COME OUT

DAMN LAURA'S HAVING MY BABY
SOMETIMES IT'S HARD TO BELIEVE
A MAN LIKE MYSELF, A FATHER
TOO EXCITING TO CONCEIVE

I'M BLESSED TO HAVE THIS OPPORTUNITY
TO BE A HUSBAND AND A FATHER
SOME MEN TAKE PRIDE IN NEITHER
BUT I FEEL THAT IT'S AN HONOR

TO HAVE A LOVING WIFE AS I DO
AND A BABY ON THE WAY
THIS IS THE MEANING OF HAPPINESS
IF I MY SELF MUST SAY

DAMN LAURA'S HAVING MY BABY
THEY MEAN SO MUCH TO ME
SPECIAL THANKS TO MY SISTER IN LAW
FOR INSPIRING THIS POETRY

MAKING A BABY

MARRIED TO EACH OTHER
SO SWEET SO FINE
MAKING PASSIONATE LOVE
WITH KNOW SINS IN MIND

HAVING ORAL SEX AND INTERCOURSE
WITH ALL THE MOISTURE AND LUST
THRUSTING AND SUCKING
WITH ONE YOU LOVE AND TRUST

SO SWEET SO FINE,
THOUGHTS WHEN I THINK OF YOU
CALLING OUT MY NAME
THE WHOLE NIGHT THROUGH

TIED UP IN PASSION
KNOW WHERE ON EARTH TO BE FOUND
HOLDING EACH OTHER TIGHTLY
TEN FEET OFF THE GROUND

HOLDING BACK THE CLIMAX
SUCH A WONDERFUL PAIN
LICKING AND TOUCHING
DRIVING EACH OTHER INSANE

I LOVE YOU LAURA, "HE SAID"
"I LOVE YOU TOO," SHE CONFESSED
IN THE MIST OF PASSION
TWO LOVERS AT THEIR BEST

ADDITIONAL LOVE

IN DECEMBER
OUR NEW FAMILY BEGUN
WE BECAME THREE MY DARLING
BUT ALWAYS BEING ONE

I VOWED MYSELF TO YOU FOREVER
AND YOU, YOURSELF TO ME
TOGETHER WE ARE THE ROOTS
OF OUR CHILDREN, CHILDREN'S FAMILY TREE

LAURA YOU'VE GIVEN ME LOVE AND HAPPINESS
MY HEART JUST WANTS TO EXPLAIN
THAT YOU ARE THE REASON FOR MY SMILE
YOU DWELL IN MY HEARTS DOMAIN

TOGETHER WE HAVE ACCOMPLISHED PLENTY
WHEN OTHERS HAVE NOT
TOGETHER WE PRACTICE LOVING ONE ANOTHER
WHEN OTHERS HAVE FORGOT

IN THE BEGINNING MONTHS OF THE YEAR
MY SMILE WILL SHINE BRIGHTER WITH GLEE
BECAUSE IN ADDITION TO LOVING YOU MORE
I'LL BE LOVING THE CHILD YOU'VE GIVEN ME

COMPREHENSION OF LIFE

IF I HAD A CHANCE TO DO
LIFE ALL OVER AGAIN
I WOULD HAVE TO DECLINE THAT 2ND CHANCE
CAN YOU COMPREHEND

2ND CHANCES CAN BE A BLESSING
ONE SHOULD RELISH IN
2ND CHANCES DON'T COME OFTEN
CAN YOU COMPREHEND

WE ALL TAKE 2ND CHANCES EVERY DAY
AS SIMPLE AS CROSSING THE STREET
AS SIMPLE AS DRINKING A GLASS OF WATER
OR CONSUMING A PIECE OF MEAT

IF I HAD A CHANCE TO DO
A DAY ALL OVER AGAIN
A DAY I HAD NO CONTROL OF
CAN YOU COMPREHEND

IF I HAD A CHANCE TO DO
WHAT I SHOULD OF DONE THEN
WOULD MY LIFE BE DIFFERENT
OR WOULD IT BE AT AN END

NEVER DWELL ON WHAT YOU SHOULD HAVE DONE
OR WHAT YOU HAD A CHANCE TO DO
DWELL ON WHAT THE FUTURE HOLDS
AND THE OPPORTUNITIES A HEAD OF YOU

LOVING YOU IN RED

RED IS THE COLOR OF LOVE
I REALIZE THAT TODAY
TOMORROW MIGHT BE ANOTHER COLOR
BUT TODAY I FEEL THIS WAY

RED IS THE COLOR OF MY HEART
THAT BEATS THE WHOLE NIGHT THROUGH
RED IS WHAT I SEE MY DARLING
WHEN I MAKE LOVE TO YOU

WITH MY EYES I SEE YOUR BEAUTY
WITH MY HEART I FEEL YOUR LOVE
WITH MY BODY I FEEL ALL THAT'S HAPPENING INSIDE OF YOU
AS WE DO EVERYTHING WE EVER DREAMED OF

MAKING LOVE TO YOU IS MORE THAN SPECIAL
I CAN DESCRIBE IT IN MANY WAYS
TODAY I MAKE LOVE TO YOU IN RED
TOMORROW IT MAY BE GRAYS

MY HEART IS SOMETIMES JEALOUS
BECAUSE, FOR ONE MOMENT IT WOULD LIKE TO SEE
YOUR BEAUTY THAT MY EYES RELISH IN
WHICH WILL LAST AN ETERNITY

LOVING YOU IN RED
IS THE WAY I FEEL TODAY
LOVING YOU FOREVER
THOSE FEELINGS WILL NEVER GO AWAY

LOVE IS ON THE PROWL

LOVE IS ON THE PROWL
IT'S STALKING ME AGAIN
DOUBLING THE WAY I FEEL FOR YOU
AS A LOVER, HUSBAND AND FRIEND

HOW CAN I LOVE YOU A SECOND TIME
MY FIRST FEELINGS HAVE NEVER CHANGED
I'LL NEVER STOP LOVING YOU MY LAURA
NOW IT'S TWICE AS WONDERFUL, YET STRANGE

IS THIS A CONTINUING PATTERN, TRUE LOVE
MULTIPLYING EVERY YEAR
REASSURANCE THAT OUR LOVE WILL NEVER END
SO WE HAVE NOTHING TO FEAR MY DEAR

I CAN FEEL THE PROWLER INSIDE OF ME
BUILDING A MONUMENT OF WHAT WE SHARE
LOVE IS THE PROWLER MY DARLING
ADDING ON TO THE LOVE THAT IS THERE

LOVE IS ON THE PROWL
STALKING ME DEEP WITHIN
LEAVING BEHIND ENOUGH LOVE IN MY HEART
UNTIL THE PROWLER STRIKES AGAIN

HAPPY BIRTHDAY

HAPPY BIRTHDAY BEAUTIFUL
YOU DESERVE EVERYTHING YOUR HEART DESIRES
THE ONLY THING THAT I CAN TRULY PROMISE
IS THE LOVE I HAVE FOR YOU
TAKING YOU HIGHER AND HIGHER

HAPPY BIRTHDAY MY WIFE AND LOVER
ANOTHER YEAR HAS COME UPON THEE
WHICH MEANS YOU'RE ANOTHER YEAR BEAUTIFUL
FULL OF LOVE THAT IS MEANT FOR ME

BABY YOU DESERVE THE BEST
AND WITH ALL MY HEART, MY KNOWLEDGE, MY STRENGTH
MY WISDOM, EVEN MY LAST BREATH
I WILL COME THROUGH FOR YOU.
I WILL LOVE YOU AND BE WITH YOU FOREVER

HAPPY HAPPY ANNIVERSARY

TWO YEARS ALREADY
OH MY! TIME FLIES
WHEN THE LOVE YOU AND I SHARE
NEVER WILTER NOR DIES

BEING MARRIED TO YOU
HAS A FANTASY EFFECT
WHEN OUR LOVE GROWS STRONGER
IN TIMES OF NEGLECT

AMAZING ENCOUNTERS
TRUE LOVE TO ADORE
THE FEELINGS WE SHARE
NEVER FELT BEFORE

IS IT A DREAM I'M DREAMING
DO DREAMS COME TRUE
CAN A MAN LOVE A WOMAN
THE WAY I LOVE YOU

HAPPY ANNIVERSARY MY LAURA
OUR MARRIAGE IS MEANT TO BE
FOREVER YOU AND I
I LOOK FORWARD TO YEAR THREE

STRONG BLACK WOMAN

STRONG BLACK WOMAN
THAT'S WHAT SHE IS
SHE CAN BRING HOME A PAY CHECK
PLEASE ME WHEN NEEDED
AND TAKE CARE OF HER KIDS

STRONG BLACK WOMAN
WHETHER SHE IS SINGLE YOUNG OR OLD
LIVING UP TO EXPECTATIONS
THAT ONLY BLACK WOMEN CAN HOLD

NEGOTIATING WITH SOCIETY
EXCELLING IN HER WORLD
SHE IS THE MOTHER OF OUR COUNTRY
AND ALSO THE MOTHER OF MY BABY GIRL

STRONG BLACK WOMAN
I WORK HARD TO GET MINE
STRONG BLACK WOMAN
A MAN COULD TAKE YEARS TO FIND

STRONG BLACK WOMAN
THAT'S EXACTLY WHAT I SEE
I WOULDN'T GIVE MINE UP
FOR NOTHING IN THE WORLD
BECAUSE SHE IS THE WORLD TO ME

MEMORY

THIS IS A DAILY REMINDER
OF HOW I LOVE YOU SO MUCH
MY LOVE FOR YOU IS INCREDIBLY STRONG
THAT I COULD USE IT AS A CRUTCH

IT CARRIES ME THROUGH THE BAD TIMES
JUST AS WELL AS THE GOOD
THIS LOVE FOR YOU INSIDE MY HEART
IS FOR YOU MY BLACK RIDING HOOD

THIS IS A DAILY REMINDER
OF HOW I THINK ABOUT YOU EVERY DAY
I THINK ABOUT YOUR SMILE AND YOUR EVERYDAY LAUGHTER
I HEAR YOU SAYING (I LOVE YOU RAY)

I'M GLAD I LOVE YOU LAURA
BECAUSE TIMES WHEN THE SUN DON'T SHINE
I CLOSE MY EYES AND PICTURE YOU
FOR YOU ARE THE SUNSHINE IN MY MIND

THIS IS A DAILY REMINDER
OF HOW I NEED YOU IN MY LIFE
AND HOW I SEEM TO LOVE YOU MORE EACH DAY
THAT'S WHY I WANT YOU TO BE MY WIFE

SHINNING DARKNESS

I'M YOUR KNIGHT IN SHINING DARKNESS
WHO MOVES THROUGH OUT THE NIGHT
I APPEAR TO BE SOMEONE DIFFERENT
TO WHOM EVER HAS ME IN SIGHT

BUT ONLY YOU CAN EXSTINGUISH THE DARKNESS
WHICH CONDEMED MY VERY SOUL
TRUE LOVE IS THE KEY TO THE LIGHT
WHAT IS DARK DREARY AND COLD

YOU ARE MY BREATH OF FRESH AIR
TO HAVE 24 HOURS A DAY
WITHOUT YOU THE DARKNESS WILL CONSUME ME
AND FILL ME WITH DISMAY

I'M YOUR KNIGHT IN SHINING DARKNESS
WHO DWELLS ON YOU THROUGH THE NIGHT
I REACH OUT FOR THE LOVE IN YOU
WHICH WILL FILL MY SOUL WITH LIGHT

I AM NO LONGER FILLED WITH DARKNESS
FOR YOU HAVE SET ME FREE
NOW I CAN LOVE AND BE LOVED
BECAUSE YOU SHINE THE LIGHT ON ME

THOUGHTS OF YOU

HELLO MY DARLING LAURA
THAT BEGINNING RINGS A BELL
OF A POEM I ONCE WROTE TO YOU
IF MY MEMORY SERVES ME WELL

IT EITHER WENT SOMETHING LIKE THIS
BETTER YET SOMETHING LIKE THAT
I'M JUST A TAD BIT CONFUSED
WITH MY MEMORY THAT'S NOT EXACT

FOR THE PAST TWO DAYS THE SUN DID NOT APPEAR
MY DESIRE TO BATHE WAS FAR FROM MY MIND
I ONLY HAD THOUGHTS OF YOU, MY DARLING
AND NOT WASHING MY BEHIND

I MISS YOU WITH A PASSION
YOU'RE MY DRUG AND I NEED A FIX
YOU'RE ALL THE INGREDIENTS I REQUIRE
WITH A TOUCH OF BROWN SUGAR IN THE MIX

ALL JOKES ASIDE
I REALLY MISS YOU AND THE BABY TOO
YOU TWO ARE MY WORLD
AND I LOVE BOTH OF YOU

TO THE BOTH OF YOU

SHOULD I TALK TO YOU LIKE AN ADULT
TREAT YOU LIKE A CHILD
GET FRUSTRATED WHEN YOU CRY TOO MUCH
LOVE YOU MORE WHEN YOU SMILE

ALL THESE DECISIONS
WHEN ONE LOVES SOMEONE LIKE YOU
WHOM I WILL PAMPER ALL DAY LONG
AND LONG FOR ALL NIGHT THROUGH

I WORRY ABOUT YOUR EATING HABITS
SO I CAN KEEP YOU HEALTHY AND STRONG
BECAUSE I WANT TO HOLD YOU CLOSE AND TIGHT
WHEN I HEAR MY FAVORITE SONG

YOU GIVE ME FEELINGS OF WARMTH
WHICH I NEVER FELT BEFORE
ARE YOU ALL I EXPECT YOU TO BE
OR MAYBE EVEN MORE

I LOVE TO TELL THE WORLD ABOUT YOU
AND I'M PROUD YOU'RE PART OF ME
TODAY IT'S YOU AND I
TOMORROW IT'S ME, YOU AND SHE

THESE WORDS ARE WORDS OF WISDOM
SOME ARE WORDS FROM THE HEART
MY WISH IS THAT WE ALWAYS REMAIN WHOLE
AND NEVER BE APART

HELLAVA WOMAN

EXPERIENCING WHAT YOU WENT THROUGH
ENHANCES MY LOVE AND RESPECT FOR YOU
NINE MONTHS OF PREGNANCY
LABOR THEN BIRTH
SHOULD ENHANCE YOUR SELF ESTEEM
AND YOUR SELF WORTH

YOUR QUITE A WOMAN LAURA
I'M GLAD YOUR MINE
COURAGEOUS AND BEAUTIFUL
FULL OF SUNSHINE
THIS IS JUST A REMINDER
OF WHAT YOU MEAN TO ME
YOU'RE THE EPITOME OF A BLACK WOMAN
AND PROUD YOU SHOULD BE

IF I'D EVER BEEN BLESSED
IN MY ENTIRE LIFE
I WAS BLESSED THE DAY
THAT YOU BECAME MY WIFE
NOW YOU'VE GIVEN ME A DAUGTHER
UNBELIVEABLE, AS IT MAY SEEM
REALITY HAS COME
AND BROUGHT TO LIFE MY DREAM

BRAVO MY DARLING
A JOB WELL DONE
BUT NEXT TIME MY LOVE
MAY I PLEASE HAVE A SON

I LOVE YOU

SHOW ME

YOU HAVE TO SHOW ME YOU LOVE ME
JUST TWO MINUTES OUT OF THE DAY
SOMETIMES I NEED MORE THAN JUST TO HEAR THE WORDS
EVEN THOUGH THEY'RE LOVELY WORDS TO SAY

FLOWERS A LETTER OR POST CARD
WHAT EVER MAY COME TO MIND
SOMETHING THAT SHOWS I'M SPECIAL
THAT TWO MINUTES A DAY AT A TIME

I'M NOT SAYING
THAT YOU DON'T LOVE ME
THE WHOLE WORLD KNOWS THAT YOU DO
I ESPECIALLY KNOW IT
THAT'S WHY I'M MARRIED TO YOU

YOU HAVE TO SHOW ME YOU LOVE ME
AND I WILL DO THE SAME FOR YOU
WE NEED SPECIAL MOMENTS IN OUR MARRIAGE
THOSE SPECIAL MOMENTS I WANT TO GIVE TO YOU

YOU HAVE TO SHOW ME YOU LOVE ME
JUST TWO MINUTES OUT OF THE DAY
SOMETIMES I NEED MORE THAN JUST TO HEAR THE WORDS
EVEN THOUGH THEY'RE LOVELY WORDS TO SAY

THE YOU KNOW

THANK YOU FOR THE YOU KNOW
IT WAS SO, SO OH SO
WONDERFUL DON'T YOU KNOW
FROM MY HEAD TO MY TOE

I CAN'T WAIT UNTIL THE TIME COMES AGAIN
WHEN THE YOU KNOW WHO KICKS IN
I REALLY MISS OUR MUTUAL FRIEND
IN AND OUT, OUT AND IN

AND WHEN DOING THE YOU KNOW
UP AND DOWN FAST AND SLOW
THE TIME WILL ALWAYS COME
WHEN YOU MAY STAY OR YOU MAY GO

LETS THANK GOD FOR THE YOU KNOW
HE GAVE US EACH OTHER HO HO HO
AND I LOVE YOU EVEN THOUGH
I LOVE YOU MORE WHEN WERE DOING THE YOU KNOW

MIDNIGHT TO EIGHT

THE SHORTEST ROAD GOES ON FOREVER
THE CLOSER I GET TO YOU
THE URGES AND DESIRES INTENSIFY
WHEN LOVE IS OVERDUE

AS I LOOK INTO MY REARVIEW MIRROR
AND MILES JUST PAST AWAY
A LOVE SONG COMES ON THE RADIO
AND ENCOURAGES WHAT I HAVE TO SAY

OH, HOW I LOVE YOU MY DEAR LAURA
THOSE WORDS THAT I WILL NEVER FORGET
AS THEY FLOW FROM MY HEART, LEAP OFF MY TONGUE
THESE WORDS ARE MOIST AND WET

THE SHORTEST ROAD GOES ON FOREVER
THE CLOSER I GET TO YOU
THE TEMPERATURE IN THE CAR BEGINS TO RISE
WITH THE FOG THAT'S NOW IN VIEW

AS I CHECK MY REARVIEW MIRROR ONCE MORE
THE WHITE LINES FADE TO BLACK
I THINK ABOUT YOU AND THE BABY
AND THE LOVE WE HAVE INTACT

OH WHAT A WONDERFUL FEELING
YOU'VE MADE ME HAPPY AND FULL OF GLEE
IN THE BEGINNING THERE WERE ONLY TWO OF US
NOW WITH THE GRACE OF GOD
THERE IS THREE

THE SHORTEST ROAD GOES ON FOREVER
WHETHER IT'S ONE LANE OR TWO
BUT I'LL TRAVEL THIS ROAD UNTIL THE END OF TIME
AS LONG AS MY DESTINATION IS YOU

THIRD ANNIVERSARY

DEAR LAURA

GOD HAS BLESSED US ONCE AGAIN MY DEAR
BY GIVEN US GUIDANCE THROUGH OUT THE YEAR
HE'S SEEN IT FIT FOR US TO BE
CELEBRATING ANNIVERSARY NUMBER THREE

LET'S CHERISH THESE PRECIOUS MOMENTS
MAY THE FEELINGS LINGER ON
LET'S FREEZE THIS NIGHT IN TIME
BECAUSE TOMORROW IT WILL BE GONE

I LOVED YOU EVER SINCE OUR WEDDING
AND MANY YEARS BEFORE
BELIEVE IT OR NOT MY DARLING LAURA
TODAY I LOVE YOU MORE

TOMORROW IS NEVER PROMISED
BUT TODAY I'M HERE TO SAY
THANK YOU FOR THREE YEARS OF LOVE AND COMFORT
FOREVER YOURS, YOUR HUSBAND RAY

HAPPY ANNIVERSARY

MERRY CHRISTMAS

MERRY XMAS MY DEAR WIFE
AND WHAT A MERRY XMAS IT WILL BE
YET ALL OUR XMASES HAVE BEEN MERRY
EVER SINCE THAT DAY YOU MARRIED ME

MAY YOU RECEIVE EVERYTHING YOU WISH FOR
MAY JOY FOLLOW WITH ALL THAT IS DEAR
MAY YOUR MARRIAGE AND MOTHERHOOD BLOSSOM
EVERY DAY THROUGHOUT THE NEW YEAR

MERRY XMAS MY DEAR LAURA
MAY WE CELEBRATE THE DAYS AHEAD
FOR YOU ARE THE LOVE OF MY LIFE ALL YEAR ROUND
SO IT WAS WRITTEN NOW LET IT BE SAID

I HAVE XMAS EVERY DAY OF THE YEAR
AND I THANK THE LORD MY GOD FOR THIS
HE BLESSED ME WITH THE GREATEST GIFT OF ALL
SO LISTEN WHILE I REMINISCE

I'VE BEEN GIVEN THE GIFT OF LOVE
SO I CAN BE LOVED
I'VE BEEN GIVEN THE GIFT OF A WIFE
THROUGH HER WE CREATED ANOTHER LIFE
I'VE BEEN GIVEN THE GIFT OF KNOWLEDGE
OF HOW TO KEEP A ROOF OVER MY HEAD
I'VE BEEN GIVEN THE GIFT OF PRAYER
SO I CANNOT BE MISLEAD

WHAT IT REALLY BOILS DOWN TO
IS THAT ALL OF MY BLESSING
STARTED WITH YOU
MERRY XMAS

JUST SAYING THANKS

HAVE I SAID THANKS TO YOU LATELY
FOR ALL YOU'VE DONE FOR ME
YOU ARE A FINANCIAL GENIUS
AND YOU LEAD ME GRACIOUSLY

YOU GAVE LIFE TO MY DAUGHTER
WHO IN RETURN SHOWED ME THE MEANING OF LIFE
HAVE I THANKED YOU LATELY MY DEAR
FOR BEING A WONDERFUL WIFE

HAVE I THANKED YOU RECENTLY
FOR ALLOWING ME TO SHOW YOU LOVE
ALONG WITH HONESTY AND FAITH
THAT I THINK HIGHLY OF

YOU WERE BORN TO BE MY LADY
I WAS BORN TO BE YOUR GENTLE MAN
TOGETHER THE LOVE WE SHARE
SHALL BE THE GREATEST IN ALL THE LAND

HAVE I SAID THANKS TO YOU LATELY
FOR ALL THE THINGS I FORGOT TO THANK YOU ABOUT
HAVE I TOLD THE WORLD HOW MUCH I LOVE YOU
IN A LOUD AND BOISTEROUS SHOUT
HAVE I HUGGED YOU WITH A PASSION
THAT WOULD MAKE YOU WHISPER IN MY EAR
ALL THE THINGS YOU WANTED TO SAY DURING ALL
OUR LOVE MAKING THE PREVIOUS YEAR

THERE'S SO MUCH I WOULD LIKE TO THANK YOU ABOUT
YET THERE'S SO LITTLE TIME
BUT THERE IS ALWAYS TIME TO SAY I LOVE YOU
EVEN THOUGH IT'S IN A RHYME

I LOVE YOU LAURA
SINCE THE SECOND TIME WE MET
MY LOVE FOR YOU HAS GROWN
AND WILL CONTINUE, YOU CAN BET

I LOVE YOU LAURA
WITH EVERY BREATH I TAKE
TOGETHER WE WILL PROSPER
FOREVER AND FOR GOODNESS SAKE

THOUGHTS OF LOVE

NO MATTER WHERE I'M AT
OR WHAT SITUATION I'M IN
MY MIND MIGHT BE THINKING OF ONE THING
BUT MY HEART WILL NEVER RESCIND

THE DEFINITION OF THIS IS
I ALWAYS LOVE YOU LAURA
WHAT EVER MY LIFE DICTATES AT THE TIME
I'LL ALWAYS LOVE YOU BECAUSE
MY HEART IS YOURS AND YOUR LOVE IS MINE

ONE SAID IN THE MIND, THOUGHTS ARE CONTINUOUS
ONE NEVER SAID ANYTHING ABOUT THE HEART
I'M SAYING MY LOVE FOR YOU IS ETERNAL
THE HEART JUST PLAYS A PART

WHAT I FEEL FOR YOU
IS BEYOND OUR THOUGHT PROCESS
WHAT I FEEL FOR YOU
WAS CONCEIVED IN ANOTHER UNIVERSE
WITH INTENSE ENERGY
EVERLASTING, FOR BETTER OR WORSE

NO MATTER WHERE I AM
OR WHETHER MY LIFE IS AT AN END
YOU WILL ALWAYS HAVE THE KEY TO MY HEART
THOUGHTS OF LOVE, YOUR HUSBAND AND YOUR FRIEND

LA FAMILE

I MISSED YOU GUYS TODAY
IN A SPECIAL KIND OF WAY
THESE FEELINGS I HAVE SEEM TO BE
ME MISSING MY NEW AND CHOSEN FAMILY

YOU TWO ARE ALL I EVER WANTED
A BEAUTIFUL WIFE AND A BEAUTIFUL CHILD
I HAVE ALL THE MORE REASON FOR LIVING
AND EVEN MORE REASON TO SMILE

THE MORE I THINK ABOUT LIFE
THE MORE IT SEEMS LIKE A WONDERFUL DREAM
AND MARRYING YOU MY DARLING LAURA
IGNITED THIS DREAM IT SEEMS

PRIOR TO YOU LIFE WAS A NIGHTMARE
WHEN DREAMING I ONLY GRIEVED
THEN YOUR SMILE SHINED UPON ME
POOF, TRUE LOVE WAS CONCEIVED

TAYLOR IS WHAT YOU NAMED HER
THROUGH OUR LOVE SHE CAME TO BE
SHE IS THE MOST GENEROUS, AND UNSELFISH GIFT
THAT YOU COULD HAVE EVER GIVEN ME

I MISSED YOU GUYS TODAY
IN THAT SPECIAL KIND OF WAY
WHICH IS NOW KNOWN TO ME
AS FEELINGS OF MISSING MY NEW FAMILY

MESSAGE

TIME IS SLOWLY CREEPING
AND THE STORK IS ON THE WAY
BUT THIS ONE DOES NOT FLY
HAS ANYONE SEEN MY STORK TODAY

SHE'S 5' 2" HER NAME IS LAURA
JUST AS BEAUTIFUL AS CAN BE
IF YOU HAPPEN TO SEE MY STORK
WILL YOU SEND HER BACK TO ME

A SECRET I'LL LET YOU IN ON
WITH THIS STORK I AM IN LOVE
WHEN I MET HER SHE HAD WINGS
AND FLEW TO ME FROM ABOVE

I'M SENDING OUT THIS MESSAGE
BECAUSE MY STORK IS ALMOST DUE
SHE'S CARRYING AROUND MY UNBORN
WITH REMAINING WEEKS A FEW

IT'S ALMOST 8 AM
AND SOON I WILL BE HOME AGAIN
THE STORK SHOULD DEFINITELY BE THERE
SEE, SHE'S ALSO MY WIFE AND FRIEND

END MESSAGE

MY BETTER HALF

LAURA YOU BROUGHT ME SO MUCH JOY AND HAPPINESS
UPON OCCASION THERES ALSO BEEN PAIN
BUT THE PAIN NEVER OUT WAY THE HAPPINESS
OR THE LOVE MY HEART CONTAINS

IF I COULD TURN HOW I FEEL INTO DOLLARS
THE WEALTH WOULD NEVER END
OUR LOVE WILL LAST FOREVER
THROUGH ELEMENTS THICK AND THIN

YOU GIVEN ME MORE STRENGTH AND CONFIDENCE
A MAN NEEDS THAT FROM HIS WIFE THESE DAYS
WITHOUT MORAL SUPPORT FROM ONE ANOTHER
A MARRIAGE ONLY DECAYS

WE HAVE AN INCREDIBLE AMOUNT OF LOVE FOR EACH OTHER
ENOUGH TO LAST THROUGH THE END OF TIME
IF ONE DAY WE CEASE TOUCHING PHYSICALLY
WE WILL ETERNALLY TOUCH THROUGH THE MINDS

DEAR LORD GIVE US THE STRENGTH TO BE ONE FOREVER
MAY WE CONTINUE TO LOVE AND CONTINUE TO LAUGH
I PRAY TO YOU EVERY NIGHT AND EVERY MORNING
    THANKING YOU
FOR SENDING ME MY BETTER HALF

HELP

YOU WANTED ME TO RELEASED FEELINGS
THAT WERE BURIED INSIDE OF ME
I WANT TO RELEASE THEM ALSO
BUT YOU HAVE TO HELP ME SET THEM FREE

YOU HAVE TO REACH INSIDE OF ME TO TOUCH ME
AND ACTIVATE WHAT'S BEEN DORMANT FOR SO LONG
YOU HAVE TO BRING OUT WHAT MOTIVATED ME
WHAT KEPT ME GOING STRONG

THOSE FEELINGS ARE UNBELIVEABLE
AND I LONG TO HAVE THEM BACK
YOU NEED TO FEEL THEM ALSO
YES THEM FEELINGS THAT YOU LACK

I'M GOING TO GIVE IT MY ALL
AND PROBABLY A LITTLE BIT MORE
WILL YOU HELP ME MY LOVE
TO BRING BACK THE FEELINGS I HAD BEFORE

EVEN THOUGH I TELL YOU I LOVE YOU
AND I MEAN IT WITH ALL MY HEART
IT'S NOT THE SAME WITHOUT THOSE FEELINGS
THAT ARE HIDING IN THE DARK

LOVED

I WISH WE WOULD'VE MET EARLIER
THEN OUR LOVE WOULD HAVE DEVELOPED SOONER
AND WE MIGHT BE LIVING TOGETHER IN A SHACK
LIKE ALICE AND RALPH ON THE HONEY MOONERS

IT DOESN'T MATTER WHERE WE ARE
I'M SURE THAT WE'D BE HAPPY
I'D LOVE YOU IF YOUR HAIR WAS LONG
AND I'D LOVE YOU IF IT WERE NAPPY

I WOULD HAVE LOVED YOU IF WE NEVER MET
BECAUSE I KNEW YOU WERE SOMEWHERE
I KNEW IN MY HEART THAT ONE DAY WE'D BE TOGETHER
AND OUR TRUE LOVE WE WOULD SHARE

I REMIND MYSELF FREQUENTLY
OF HOW LUCKY I MUST BE
TO LOVE A WOMAN SUCH AS YOU
AND TO HAVE YOU LOVE A MAN LIKE ME

NOW I WISH WE STAY TOGETHER FOREVER
AND LET NO ONE AND NOTHING TEAR US APART
WITHOUT YOU MY EMOTIONS WOULD COME TO AN END
WITHOUT YOU I HAVE NO HEART

MARRIAGE IS WHAT YOU MAKE IT

MARRIAGE IS WHAT YOU MAKE IT
I'VE MADE MINE WONDERFUL FOR ME
OF COURSE WE HAVE OUR UPS AND DOWNS
BUT THAT'S NORMALITY

NOW AND THEN SHE GETS ANGRY AT ME
OTHER TIMES I GET ANGRY AT HER
BUT IT'S ALWAYS FUN WHEN WE MAKE UP
AND WHOOPEE IS ABOUT TO OCCUR

I REALLY LOVE OUR MARRIAGE
I LOVE MY WIFE AS WELL
WHEN TIMES ARE LOW AND I FEEL LIKE LEAVING
MY HEART JUST RINGS A BELL

IT REMINDS ME OF HOW MUCH SHE MEANS TO ME
AND HOW MUCH I LOVE HER SO
MY HEART THEN TAPS ME ON THE SHOULDER AND WHISPERS
YOU'LL BE A FOOL TO LET HER GO

MARRIAGE IS WHAT YOU MAKE IT
AND WERE MAKING OURS INTO GOLD
I LOVE MY WIFE WITH ALL MY HEART
AND I WILL LOVE HER MORE AS I GROW OLD

MISSING ANGEL

HEAVEN IS MISSING AN ANGEL
SHE FELL TO ME FROM THE SKY
I KNOW IT WAS A GIFT FROM GOD
SO I NEVER QUESTIONED WHY

I CAN'T IMAGINE LIFE WITHOUT HER
BECAUSE I LOVE HER VERY, VERY MUCH
I'D JUST GO CRAZY IF I COULDN'T SEE HER
OR FEEL HER TENDER TOUCH

MY LIFE HAS CHANGED TOTALLY
AND THAT IS SOMETHING I WOULD NEVER REGRET
BECAUSE THE MORE I FEEL I LOVE HER
THE BETTER MY LIFE GETS

HEAVEN IS MISSING AN ANGEL
SHE CAME TO ME OUT OF THE BLUE
I WOULDN'T TRADE HER FOR FIFTEEN ANGELS
I LOVE THIS ONE WHICH IS YOU

WEATHER ON MY MIND

WHAT IS IT ABOUT THE RAIN
THAT MAKES IT HARD TO CONTAIN
THE ONCE EMOTIONAL STRAIN
THAT IN MY BRAIN REMAINS

WHAT IS IT ABOUT THE WIND
THAT I'M UNABLE TO COMPREHEND
IN MY MIND I GO OVER AND OVER AGAIN
WHAT IS IT ABOUT THE WIND

WHAT IS IT ABOUT THE THUNDER
THAT MAKES YOU WANT TO WONDER
ABOUT LIFE'S BLEEPS AND BLUNDERS
AND ALL OF LIFE'S PRESSURES WERE UNDER

NOW WE HAVE THE SUN
THE SUN IS NUMBER ONE
IT ENHANCES WHAT LIFE'S BEGUN
I'M GLAD WE HAVE THE SUN

THANKS TO NATURE WE HAVE FOUR SEASONS
AND ALL FOUR SEASONS HAVE THEIR REASONS
THANKS TO GOD FOR MY BEAUTIFUL WIFE
WHO BROUGHT ALL FOUR SEASONS TO MY LIFE
WINTER SPRING SUMMER FALL
WITHOUT HER MEANS NOTHING AT ALL

MY NUBIAN PRINCESS

MY WIFE AND NUBIAN PRINCESS
YOUR BEAUTY STILLS GROWS STRONG
YOU STILL OBTAIN A SPARKLE IN YOUR EYE
WHEN I BEGIN TO TURN YOU ON

I ENHANCE YOUR HORMONAL BALANCE
YOUR PLEASURES BEGIN TO RISE
WE BEGIN OUR SEXUAL INTERCOURSE
LIKE A VIGOROUS EXERCISE

TINY ERUPTIONS OF PLEASURE I BEQUEATH YOU
FROM THE INNER DESIRES OF MY SOUL
AS OUR BODIES BEGIN TO CLIMAX
WE INVOLUNTARILY FORFEIT CONTROL

YOU ARE A BROWN FLAMING DESIRE OF PASSION
WHICH IGNITES ME OVER AND OVER AGAIN
MY NUBIAN WOMAN IF I COULD JUMP INSIDE OF YOU
OUR LOVE MAKING WOULD NEVER END

TODAY IS THE DAY MY NUBIAN PRINCESS
IT IS TIME FOR YOU AND I TO MATE
I KNOW YOU'RE READY AND WILLING
SO I PROMISE I WON'T BE LATE

THREE MONTHS OF MARRIAGE

EVERYONE HAS THEIR UPS AND DOWNS
AND OUR HAVE JUST BEGUN
GOD KNOWS WHAT LIES AHEAD OF US
BUT WE SHALL OVER COME

WE KNOW THAT I'M NOT PERFECT
BUT I SHALL GIVE YOU MY BEST SHOT
I'LL EVEN GIVE YOU MORE OF ME
BECAUSE LEAVING YOU I SHALL NOT

WE'VE BEEN MARRIED FOR THREE MONTHS
AND I WOULDN'T TRADE IT FOR ANYTHING IN THE WORLD
YOU HAVE NOT JUST BEEN A WONDERFUL WIFE
AND A GREAT LOVER
YOU'VE ALSO BEEN MY GIRL

SOMEONE THAT I CAN TALK TO AND TRUST
SOMEONE THAT I CAN LOVE TO THE VERY END
I KNEW IT WOULD BE GREAT BEING MARRIED TO YOU
BECAUSE I LOVE YOU AS A WIFE SHOULD BE LOVED
AND EVEN MORE
I LOVE YOU AS A FRIEND

PLACES IN THE HEART

I KNOW A PLACE OF YOURS
WHERE THE SUN DON'T SHINE
I KNOW A PLACE OF YOURS
THAT'S ALWAYS ON MY MIND

THAT PLACE OF YOURS
ALWAYS OVERWHELMS ME
EVEN THOUGH IT'S ON MY MIND CONTINOUSLY
I KNOW THAT PLACE

I KNOW THAT PLACE OF YOURS
IT PULSATES TO A SEDUCTIVE RHYTHM
EVEN BETTER, IN THAT PLACE OF YOURS
FLUIDS FLOW LIKE A SWING PENDULUM

I KNOW THAT PLACE OF YOURS
SENDS CHILLS UP AND DOWN MY SPINE
HERE I GO REMINISCING AGAIN
ABOUT YOUR PLACE, WHICH IS'NT HARD TO FIND

I KNOW A PLACE OF YOURS
WHERE OUR LOVE FREQUENTLY GROWS
AND INDEED THAT PLACE, MY LAURA
IS THE REASON I LOVE YOU SO

I KNOW THAT PLACE OF YOURS, MY DEAR
IS WHERE OUR LOVE GOT ITS START
THAT'S WHY THAT PLACE OF YOURS
IS NO OTHER THAN YOUR HEART

MY HEART LOVES YOUR HEART

HAPPY MOTHER'S DAY LAURA

HAPPY MOTHER'S DAY HONEY
FROM THE DEEPEST PART OF MY HEART
MAY I SAY THAT I'M HONORED
THAT YOU CHOSE ME TO TAKE PART

IN MAKING YOU A MOTHER
BY HELPING YOU CONCEIVE
I ENJOYED EVERY MOMENT
AND NOW IT'S HARD TO BELIEVE

THAT WE HAVE A BEAUTIFUL BABY GIRL
WITH SKIN AS SOFT AS A DOVE
A GLAMOROUS SMILE, A TAD BIT CHUBBY
WHICH MEANS THERE'S MORE OF HER TO LOVE

TODAY IS YOUR DAY
YOU'RE NOW PART OF THE ELITE
YOU JOINED THE MOTHER'S DAY CLUB
SO ENJOY IT MY SWEET

HAPPY MOTHER'S DAY

FROM YOUR HUSBAND RAY

HAPPY FIRST ANNIVERSARY

HAPPY ANNIVERSARY MRS. JONES
OUR MARRIAGE HAS SURVIVED
THE FIRST YEAR OF TESTS
WITH GODS HELP WE WILL ALWAYS BE TOGETHER
MRS. J.O.N.E.S.

I FEEL THAT MY LOVE FOR YOU
IS CONTINUING TO GROW STRONGER
AS TIME JUST PASSES AWAY
BELIEVE IT OR NOT, IF DAD COULD AFFORD IT
I'D MARRY YOU EVERYDAY

IT'S TIME TO PUMP UP THE VOLUME
A NEW YEAR IS ABOUT TO START
REMEMBER I WILL ALWAYS LOVE YOU
YOU WERE BORN WITH THE KEY TO MY HEART

HAPPY ANNIVERSARY AGAIN MY LOVELY WIFE LAURA
I CAN'T BELIEVE THIS IS NUMBER ONE
TIME FLIES WHEN YOU'RE HAPPY, IN LOVE
AND ALSO WHEN YOU'RE HAVING FUN

YOUR FIRST AND LAST HUSBAND RAY

I CAN'T IMAGINE THIS PAST YEAR NOT BEING MARRIED
IT'S AS IF MY LIFE HAS JUST BEGUN
YOU'VE MADE ME THE HAPPIEST MAN IN THE WORLD
HERE'S A TOAST TO ANNIVERSARY NUMBER ONE

IT'S YOUR SHOWER

IT'S YOUR SHOWER
AND I'M PROUD TO SAY
THAT I AM THE FATHER TO BE
OF THIS SHOWER TODAY

IT'S YOUR SHOWER LAURA
MY DARLING DEAR
ENJOY IT TO THE FULLEST
BECAUSE THE TIME IS NEAR

A SHOWER
FOR THE MOTHER TO BE
TO CELEBRATE THE NEW LIFE
WITH CLOSE FRIENDS AND FAMILY

THERE'S ONLY ONE OCCASION
WHERE HAPPINESS OVERWHELMED MY LIFE
THAT'S WHEN YOU AND I MY DARLING
BECAME HUSBAND AND WIFE

I LOVE YOU FOR WHAT YOU'RE GOING THROUGH
AND PART OF IT IS BECAUSE OF ME
SO I THANK YOU MY LOVELY WIFE LAURA
FOR ALWAYS MAKING ME AS HAPPY AS I CAN BE

3 WEEKS AWAY

IT'S HARD TO BELIEVE
THAT YOU'RE CARRYING MY CHILD
A LITTLE PERSON INSIDE OF YOU
THAT PROBABLY HAS MY SMILE

A LITTLE GIRL AS FAR AS WE KNOW
READY TO TAKE HER FIRST BREATH
BORN IN THE DIRECTION OF, TWO LOVING PEOPLE
THAT WILL LOVE HER TO DEATH

IT'S AMAZING TO ME
TO LOVE YOU LIKE I DO
WANTING TO BE WITH YOU FOREVER
NO MATTER WHAT LIFE PUTS US THROUGH

YOU'RE MORE THAN JUST A WOMAN
YOU'RE PART OF GOD HIMSELF
AS YOU'RE ABOUT TO GIVE LIFE
WITH LITTLE CONCERN FOR YOURSELF

I AM CONCERN FOR YOU
AND I WILL FEEL YOU'RE PAIN
FOR YOU AND I ARE ONE
FOREVER WE WILL REMAIN

IT'S HARD TO BELIEVE
THAT YOU'RE CARRYING MY CHILD
A LITTLE GIRL INSIDE OF YOU
THAT PROBABLY HAS YOUR SMILE

HAPPY B-DAY

HAPPY B-DAY ONCE AGAIN
MY ETERNAL WIFE
AND DEVOTED FRIEND

TODAY YOU TURNED 27
NEXT YEAR YOU'LL BE 28
AFTER THAT YOU'LL BE 29
BIG 3 OH AIN'T LIFE GREAT

DON'T LOOK AT IT AS GETTING OLDER
YOU'RE GETTING YOUNGER CAN'T YOU SEE
TODAY IS YOU'RE FIRST BIRTHDAY
AS A WIFE FOR LITTLE OLD ME

HAPPY BIRTHDAY HONEY

MOM TO BE

ARE YOU READY TO BE A MOM
WERE YOU READY TO BE MY WIFE
CAN YOU HANDLE ALL THESE RESPONSIBILITIES
FOR THE REST OF YOUR LIFE

DON'T TAKE IT UPON YOUR SELF MY LOVE
BECAUSE I'M HERE FOR YOU
TOGETHER WE WILL OVERCOME
WHAT LIFE WILL PUT US THROUGH

WE'VE NEVER BEEN PARENTS BEFORE
BUT SOMEHOW SOMEWAY
WE WILL GUIDE OUR CHILDREN THROUGH ETERNITY
BY BEGINNING ON THEIR BIRTHDAY

I LOVE THE WAY I FEEL ABOUT YOU
AND THAT MAKES ME LOVE YOU MORE
WHAT WE HAVE IS VERY SPECIAL
THESE FEELING WE SHARE AND ADORE

YOU WILL MAKE A PERFECT MOTHER
THIS I SAY WITH PRIDE
YOU ARE MY PERFECT WIFE
AND WERE A PERFECT BRIDE

YOUR HUSBAND

www.ingramcontent.com/pod-product-compliance
Lightning Source LLC
Chambersburg PA
CBHW021451240626
47154CB00005B/1796